ar
ANDReW
The Magic Violin

by Christine Platt
illustrated by Junissa Bianda

Calico Kid
An Imprint of Magic Wagon
abdobooks.com

About the Author
Christine A. Platt is an author and scholar of African and African-American history. A beloved storyteller of the African diaspora, Christine enjoys writing historical fiction and non-fiction for people of all ages. You can learn more about her and her work at christineaplatt.com.

For Nalah Palmer, Dr. Megan Yanik, and CHAW DC. —CP

To my number one supporter, Krisna Aditya. —JB

abdobooks.com

THIS BOOK CONTAINS
RECYCLED MATERIALS

Written by Christine Platt
Illustrated by Junissa Bianda
Edited by Tamara L. Britton
Art Directed by Candice Keimig

Library of Congress Control Number: 2019942283

Publisher's Cataloging-in-Publication Data

Names: Platt, Christine, author. | Bianda, Junissa, illustrator.
Title: The magic violin / by Christine Platt ; illustrated by Junissa Bianda.
Description: Minneapolis, Minnesota : Magic Wagon, 2020. | Series: Ana & Andrew
Summary: Ana & Andrew are learning to play the violin! They are excited to join the youth orchestra. At first it is fun. But when they start to lose interest, Ana & Andrew learn from an important African American about the importance of practicing.
Identifiers: ISBN 9781532136375 (lib. bdg.) | ISBN 9781644942611 (pbk.) | ISBN 9781532136979 (ebook) | ISBN 9781532137273 (Read-to-Me ebook)
Subjects: LCSH: African American families--Juvenile fiction. | Violin players--Juvenile fiction. | Music and children--Juvenile fiction. | Musical instruction--Juvenile fiction. | Practicing (Music)--Juvenile fiction. | Ancestry--Juvenile fiction.
Classification: DDC [E]--dc23

Table of Contents

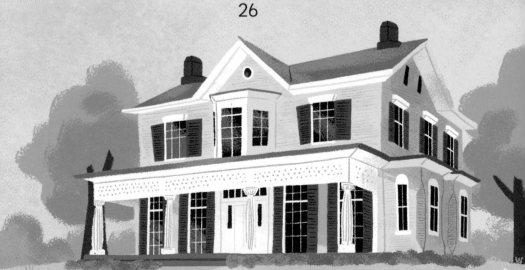

Chapter #1
The Arts Center

Every Thursday evening, Ana and Andrew went to the Arts Center with their parents. They sang songs and played games with other families. Afterward, everyone ate pizza.

Ms. Jones was the director of the Arts Center. She was very nice. One evening Ms. Jones said, "I have a special announcement." Everyone settled into their seats to listen. Sissy, Ana's favorite dolly, sat on her lap and listened too.

"The Arts Center is starting a youth orchestra and we want you to be a part of it!" Ms. Jones smiled.

"Oh, boy!" Ana shouted. "I love music!"

"Me too!" Andrew stood up and did a wiggle dance. Everyone laughed.

"And now, the most exciting part— selecting your instrument!" Ms. Jones asked everyone to follow her to the main room.

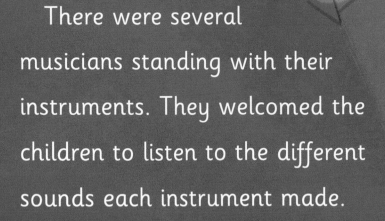

There were several
musicians standing with their
instruments. They welcomed the
children to listen to the different
sounds each instrument made.

"I hope you find the perfect
instrument!" Mama and Papa
encouraged.

EXIT

Ana and Andrew listened to the drum. "That sounds like thunder," Andrew said.

Next, they listened to the flute. "It sounds like birds singing." Ana smiled.

Then, Ana and Andrew listened to a musician play the violin. They looked at each other and smiled.

"We want to play the violin!" Ana and Andrew said excitedly.

Ms. Jones handed Ana and Andrew their violins. "I look forward to our first lesson."

"Me too," Andrew said.

"Me and Sissy too!" Ana shouted.

Chapter #2
Practice, Practice

Being a member of the youth
orchestra was a big responsibility.
Ana and Andrew had to take care of
their violins. They also had to keep
their sheet music neat and organized.
But most importantly, every day
they had to practice.

"Practice, practice, practice!"
Andrew complained. "I'm tired of
practicing."

Ana hugged Sissy close. "Me and Sissy are tired too."

"Can we skip practicing today and play instead?" Andrew asked Papa. "Please?"

"Yes," Ana agreed. "Just this one day? Pretty please?"

"You wanted to join the youth orchestra," Papa reminded Ana and Andrew. "And you promised to practice every day. That was the commitment you made to Ms. Jones and the other orchestra members."

"What's a commitment?" Ana wanted to know.

"It's promising to do what you said, like practicing, even when you don't want to," Papa explained.

"But playing the violin is hard," Andrew said. "I want to make music but all I do is make squeaks."

"All I do is squeak too." Ana ran her bow across the violin strings. "Squeaky like a mouse!"

Papa laughed. "Everyone squeaks unless they practice!"

Ana and Andrew sighed.

"Have a seat," Papa said. "Many years ago, there was a famous man who lived in Washington, DC. He squeaked on his violin until he learned to make music. In fact, he practiced so much that people thought his violin was made of magic. That's how beautifully he played."

"Really?" Ana and Andrew asked.

"Oh yes," Papa said. "I'll tell you all about him, but only if you promise to practice after the story."

"We promise!" Ana and Andrew said.

"Okay." Papa smiled. "Let me tell you about Frederick Douglass and his magic violin."

Chapter #3
Magic
Mr. Douglass

"Did you say Frederick Douglass?" Andrew asked. "I learned about him in school!"

Andrew thought about his lesson. Frederick Douglass was born in Maryland. That was very close to Washington, DC, where Ana and Andrew live.

Douglass escaped slavery and later became an abolitionist, a person who worked to end slavery. But Andrew didn't remember his teacher mentioning Frederick Douglass played the violin.

"Frederick Douglass is a very famous historical figure," Papa explained. "And he did so many extraordinary things that playing the violin is often forgotten."

"In school, I learned that slaves weren't allowed to read and write," Ana said.

"Right," Andrew agreed. "There were a lot of things that slaves couldn't do. How did Frederick Douglass learn to play the violin?"

"That is a very good question,"
Papa said. "And that's what made his
violin so magical."

Ana and Andrew leaned in closer.

"Frederick Douglass taught
himself how to play the violin," Papa
explained.

"He did?" Andrew shouted.

"Wow!" Ana was very impressed.

"Yes, he practiced until he could make the most beautiful music. And whenever his friends visited his house in Washington, DC, they asked Frederick Douglass to play his magic violin."

"My violin is magic," Ana said. "I want to practice until I can make beautiful music too!"

Andrew did a wiggle dance. "Let's do it! Let's practice."

Chapter #4
The Big Recital

Ana and Andrew told the youth orchestra about Frederick Douglass and his magic violin. He inspired Ana and Andrew to practice every day. Soon, they were able to make beautiful music on their violins. The first song they learned to play was "Twinkle, Twinkle Little Star."

"Would you like to play a duet at the youth orchestra's first recital?" Ms. Jones asked.

"Absolutely!" Andrew said.

"Yes, we would love to!" Ana hugged Sissy.

No one knew where the big recital was going to be held. Ms. Jones said it was a surprise.

The day before the recital, Ms. Jones said, "Ana and Andrew told us the amazing story about Frederick Douglass and his magic violin. And to honor him, the youth orchestra's first recital will be held at his historic home in Washington, DC!"

"Really?" Ana kissed Sissy.

"Oh boy!" Andrew did a wiggle dance.

Everyone dressed up for the big recital. Sissy did too. After playing several songs with the youth orchestra, it was time for Ana and Andrew's duet. They stood on the lawn of Frederick Douglass's home and felt very special as they made beautiful music on their violins.

Ana and Andrew knew Frederick Douglass would be proud.